Becka and the Big Bubble

Becka goes to Chicago

**by Gretchen Schomer Wendel and
Adam Anthony Schomer**

Illustrated by Damon Renthrope

www.bbBubble.com

Watch and listen to
Becka online

Your free animated
Beckasodes

www.bbBubble.com

for Tony and Helen

ISBN 978-1-933754-52-9

Printed in China

Waterside Press

Becka and the Big Bubble
PO Box 230437
Encinitas, CA 92023-0437

www.bbBubble.com

A special thanks to Michelle McBride

Becka closed her eyes
And imagined what to do
She blew and blew
And blew and blew...

Flippity-Free
High-five in the flow

Onward big bubble
To Chicago!

Over Lake Michigan, two friends in flight
"Look it's Sears Tower, oh what a sight!"

Toward Buckingham Fountain, lit up with color
Splish, splash, more bubbles around her.

The fountain spurted
And their bubble popped!
They splashed on down
Drippity-Drop!

It's the **WINDY CITY** so they spread out wide
"Lickety-Split our clothes have dried!"

To Millenium Park, a magnificent sight
The Bean is so shiny and brilliantly bright.

On Navy Pier, it's a ferris wheel
Spinning for hours, "Oh, what a deal!"

Boats on the lake, gliding with beauty
Even small sailboats, "Hey that one's a cutie!"

Then the land shook, what could it be?
"Planes doing tricks...Yippity-Yee!"

They hopped on the El to ride around town
Saw a cool jazz band boogying down.

Off in the distance, a stadium so grand
Baseball at Wrigley, "I'm already a fan."

Ben caught a ball and was on TV
"Everyone's eyes are on you and me!"

The huge water tower, like a castle from the past
When all others faded this one did last.

Look at the horses, it's here that they stop
And tons of people come here to shop.

Studios and theaters, each one unique
Comedies and plays, sometimes in the street.

Just let go of fear, it's an improvised show
"We make up characters and each line as we go."

To the Taste of Chicago, a food fest outside
As if eating lunch is a carnival ride.

Monster hot-dogs, grilled corn at the stands
Chicago style pizza, "As thick as my hand!"

Throughout Grant Park, walk, bike and play
Like Dad says, "It's a family day."
A free orchestra that plays outdoors
Art and nature, museums and more.

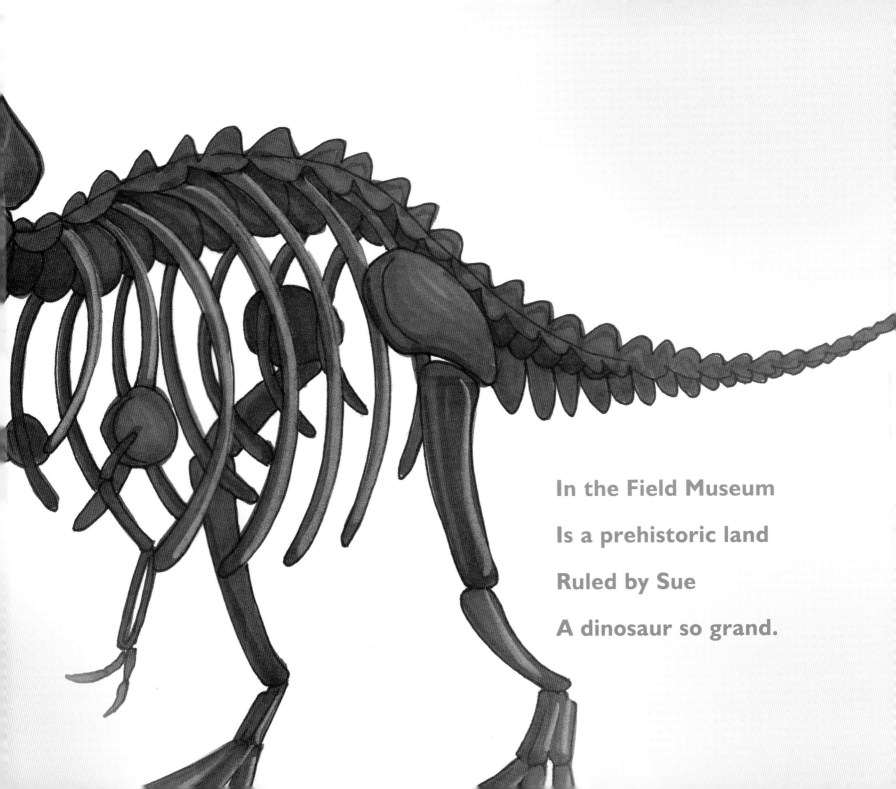

In the Field Museum

Is a prehistoric land

Ruled by Sue

A dinosaur so grand.

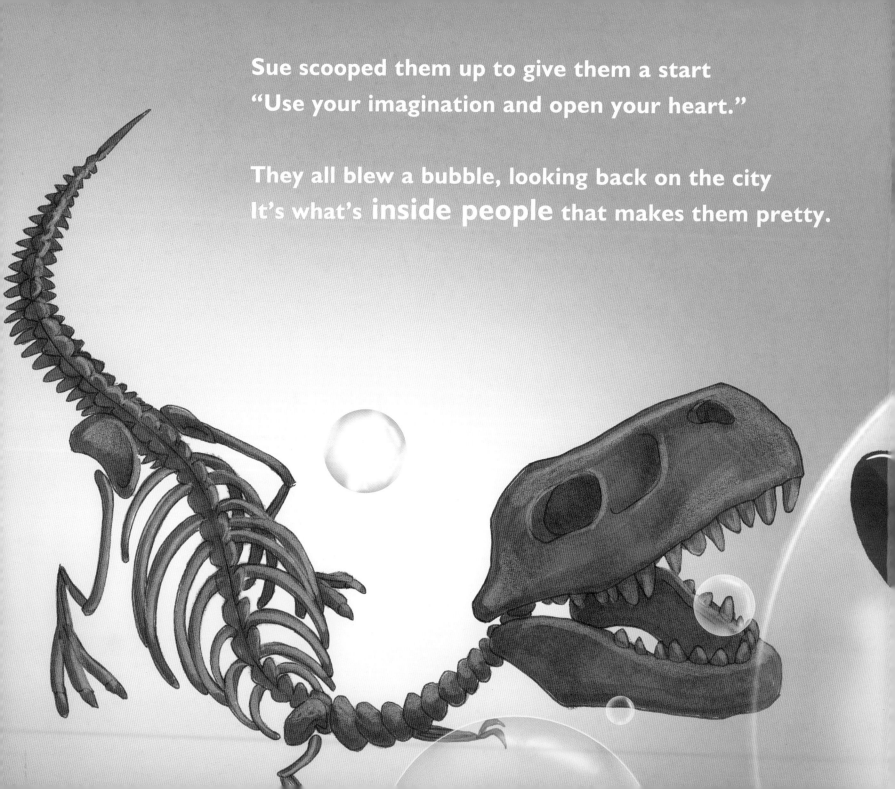

Sue scooped them up to give them a start
"Use your imagination and open your heart."

They all blew a bubble, looking back on the city
It's what's **inside people** that makes them pretty.

Goodbye Chicago, theater, fountains and pizza

"See you my friends, so nice to meet ya!"

And before they knew it

They could see Mom and Dad

And the people from town,

"You're home! We're so glad!"

Pippity-Pop!

With the flick of her nail

To the ground they sailed...

What a day it had been!